W9-BYY-721

It's Probably Penny

written and illustrated by
Loreen Leedy

Henry Holt and Company • New York

For my husband, Andy, definitely

Henry Holt and Company, LLC
Publishers since 1866
175 Fifth Avenue
New York, New York 10010
www.henryholtchildrensbooks.com

Henry Holt® is a registered trademark of Henry Holt and Company, LLC.
Copyright © 2007 by Loreen Leedy
All rights reserved.
Distributed in Canada by H. B. Fenn and Company Ltd.

Library of Congress Cataloging-in-Publication Data
Leedy, Loreen.
It's probably Penny / written and illustrated by Loreen Leedy.—1st ed.
p.   cm.
ISBN-13: 978-0-8050-7389-8 / ISBN-10: 0-8050-7389-2
1. Probabilities—Juvenile literature. I. Title.
QA273.16.L44 2007   519.2—dc22   2006002872

First Edition—2007
Printed in China on acid-free paper. ∞
10 9 8 7 6 5 4 3 2 1

My name is Lisa. We're writing down what our teacher might wear today. But I think he has a surprise for us.

What will Mr. Jayson wear today?
Write your predictions below:

a shirt

pants

a tie

socks

He is wearing a totally silly hat! "I don't usually wear hats," he says. "But as you can see, it is **possible**." He has to take it off because we can't stop laughing.

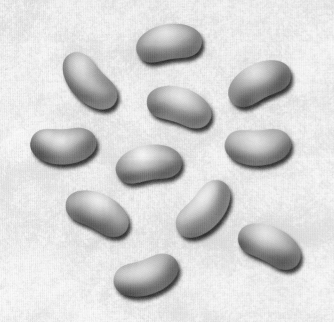

Mr. Jayson puts some jelly beans on the table. He closes his eyes and asks, "Do you predict I can pick a green one?" We say he **will** for sure because all the jelly beans are green. He picks one and then he eats it!

He makes a group with just a few green ones. So we say he **might** be able to get a green jelly bean.

We make sure his eyes are really closed. He picks a red and eats that one, too.

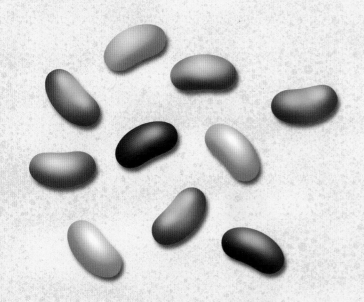

The next bunch has zero green ones, so we say he **can't** pick any green jelly beans—it's **impossible!** He tries anyway and gets an orange one. (Mr. Jayson must be hungry.)

The next group has lots of jelly beans but just one green. We predict there is only a **tiny** chance he can pick green. He gets purple and says it tastes like grapes.

This set has one of each color. Mr. Jayson asks, "What chance is there of picking green?" We say it is one out of five because there is an **equal** chance to get each color. He picks black.

The last group has three greens, one red, two oranges, and four purples. So the chances of getting each color are **unequal**. He asks us, "Which color has the highest chance of being picked?" We say purple because there are four purples out of ten jelly beans in all. But he gets a green one, at last!

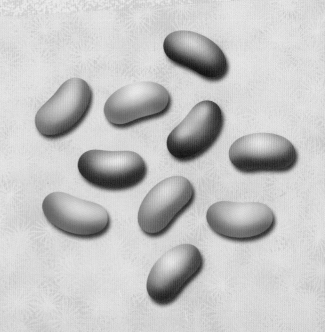

Somebody asks, "Why are we doing all this?" Mr. Jayson smiles and says it has to do with our homework for the weekend. We all groan. But he lets us eat the rest of the jelly beans, so that helps.

Probability Homework (due Monday!)

Remember to write down your predictions first, then find out the result and record it.

1) WILL, MIGHT, CAN'T
   Predict three events for this weekend:
   One that WILL happen.
   One that MIGHT happen.
   One that CAN'T happen.

2) TINY Chance or IMPOSSIBLE?
   Think of two different events.
   One has a TINY chance of happening.
   One is IMPOSSIBLE.
   Explain why they can or can't happen.

3) EQUAL Chances
   Write about an event that has three or more EQUALLY possible outcomes.

4) UNEQUAL Chances
   Tell about an event with several possible outcomes that are NOT equally likely.
   Put them in order from the MOST likely to happen to the LEAST likely.

It's a good thing we have the whole weekend.

My friend Rosa says, "I predict you're going to use your dog Penny."

"Probably," I reply.

I'm going to start as soon as
I get home. I have to think of
something that **will** happen.
I'm sure Penny will want to
go on a walk.

I need to predict an event that
might happen. When we go on a walk,
Penny usually sees a squirrel and starts barking.

Then I have to predict something that **can't** happen. That's easy! We can't see a shark because the ocean is fifty miles away.

1) WILL, MIGHT, CAN'T

Predict three events this weekend:

One that WILL happen.
One that MIGHT happen.
One that CAN'T happen.

I Predict:	Results:	
---	Right	Wrong
Penny WILL want to go on a walk.		
She MIGHT bark at a squirrel.		
We CAN'T see a shark.		

Now let's see what really happens. Do you want to go on a walk, Penny?

I knew you would. I can check off the first one.

And here is a squirrel you can bark at. It's going away, so **SHHH!**

We had a nice walk, and we didn't see a single shark.
What are you doing now, Penny?

No, a toy shark does not count. I meant a real one. Let's go inside now and have a snack.

I Predict:	Results: Right	Wrong
Penny WILL want to go on a walk.	✓	
She MIGHT bark at a squirrel.	✓	
We CAN'T see a shark.	✓	

I know how to make the perfect PB&J sandwich, with just the right amount of peanut butter and jelly. Oops, the doorbell is ringing.

I was gone for only a minute. Who has my PB&J?

It isn't my mom. She doesn't like peanut butter.

Maybe it's Spotty from next door. He sneaks inside sometimes, and once he got my cookie.

But it's **probably** Penny.

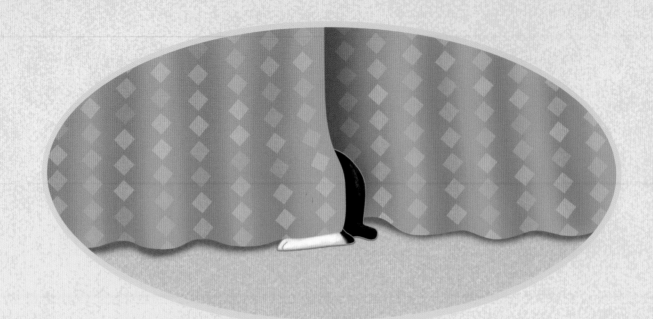

Hey, you behind the curtains. Come out of there!
Penny is eating my sandwich, all right.

Her tongue is stuck to
the roof of her mouth.
Silly girl! I'll just make
myself another one.

Now I need to think of an event with a **tiny** chance of happening. Since Penny likes people food, maybe she could eat a whole birthday cake at one time. (But she would probably get too full to finish it.)

2) TINY Chance or IMPOSSIBLE?

Think of two different events:

One has a TINY chance of happening. The other is IMPOSSIBLE (it can't ever happen).

Explain why the first event is possible but very unlikely and the other one is impossible.

If we went to the beach, there is a **tiny** chance Penny could dig up a treasure chest. A pirate could have buried it in the sand a long time ago.

But it's only a teensy-weensy chance because even if there was buried treasure somebody else has probably found it already.

Okay, my brain is getting tired. I'm going to say that Penny has a **tiny** chance to become a movie star. Some dogs have, like Lassie, but it isn't easy.

There's a TINY chance that Penny could become a movie star. Only a few dogs have been so lucky, and they know a lot more tricks than she does.

Now I'm going to think of some **impossible** events. This will be fun!

Penny will never turn into a cat. That's really **impossible**.

And she can't invent a jet pack to fly around with.

And Penny will never be the president of the United States. She couldn't even vote for herself, because dogs can't vote.

She wouldn't like being in an office all day anyway.

It is IMPOSSIBLE for Penny to be president of the United States. It can't happen because only a person can be president.

That's enough homework for tonight. We're having pizza for dinner, then we're watching a dinosaur movie.

It's time to get ready for bed.
Hey, my stuffed bunny is missing!
Who is the rabbit-napper?

Dad likes to play jokes on me. He **could** have snuck in here and hidden Bunzie.

Or Mom **might** have taken Bunzie to sew up that hole in her toe.

But it's **probably** Penny! Where are you?

You found Bunzie! Dad did the wash today, so he must have put her in, too.

I'm sorry I blamed you, Penny. You're a good girl. Let's all go to bed.

Wake up, everybody. Hey, every Saturday, Mom makes pancakes with apples, blueberries, or strawberries in them. There is an **equal** chance for each one, but I hope she is making blueberry.

3) EQUAL Chances
Write about an event that has at least three equally possible outcomes.
Mom makes 3 kinds of pancakes. I predict she'll make blueberry this morning.

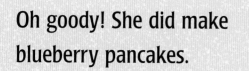

Oh goody! She did make blueberry pancakes.

Don't worry, Penny. I'll make sure there are leftovers.

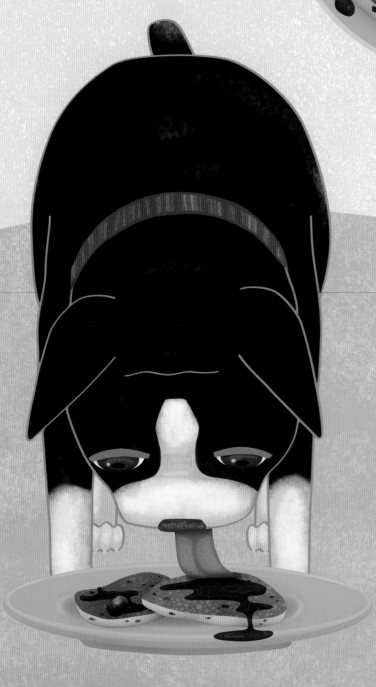

Results:
___ Apple
✓ Blueberry
___ Strawberry

We're going to the farmer's market. We go almost every weekend to get fruit and veggies and bread and a lot more, too.

This booth has a grab bag game that I can use for my homework.

4) UNEQUAL Chances
Tell about an event with several possible outcomes that are NOT equally likely. Predict the order from MOST likely to LEAST likely.

There are 10 bags in the grab bag game. The lady in the booth says there is one bag with a mini bear, five bags with candy, and four with cookies. So here are the chances when you pick a bag:

Most likely: candy (5 bags)
Next most likely: cookie (4 bags)
Least likely: mini bear (1 bag)

I know the mini bear is the **least likely** prize I'll pick, but it's worth a try.

Oh well, I got some candy, which is not a surprise.

No, Penny, you can't have any. Besides, you don't like this kind, remember?

So my homework is done already! What can I do for the rest of the weekend? I think I **will** play dress-up with Penny.

And we **might** go canoeing.

We **can't** go riding because Penny is afraid of horses.

Hey, what is that noise? It sounds like popcorn popping or firecrackers exploding or a giant mouse squeaking or a bear growling, but . . .

. . . it's **probably** Penny!